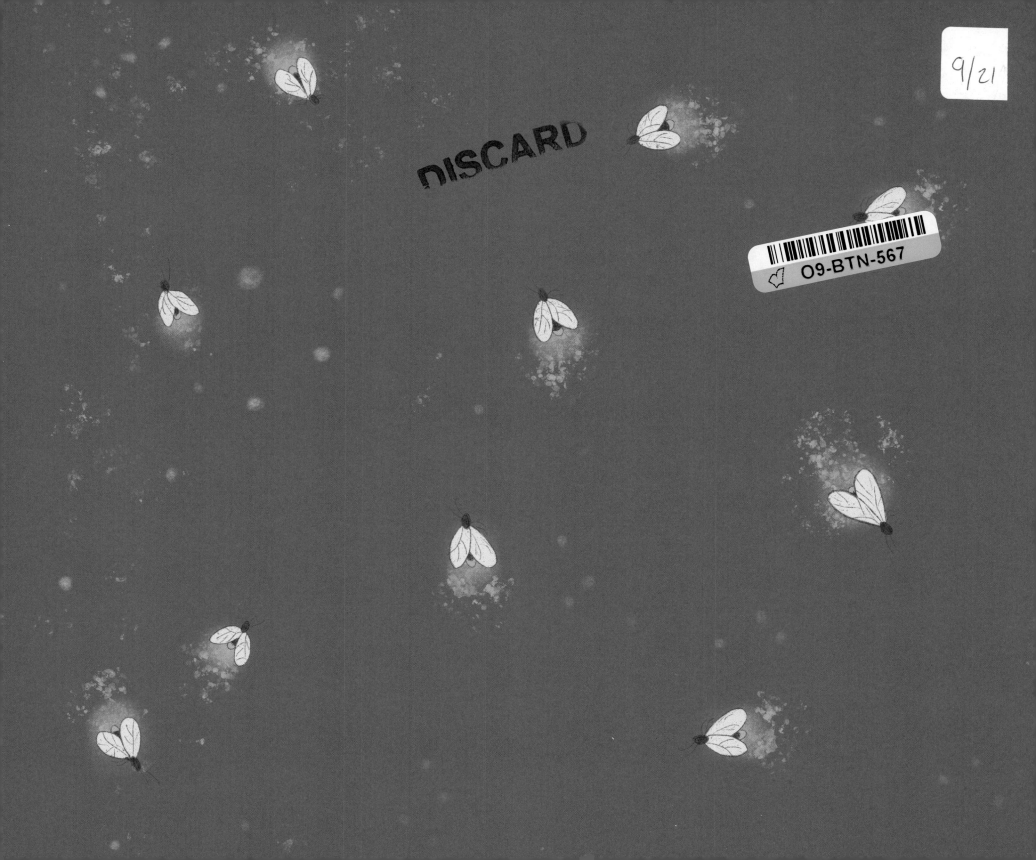

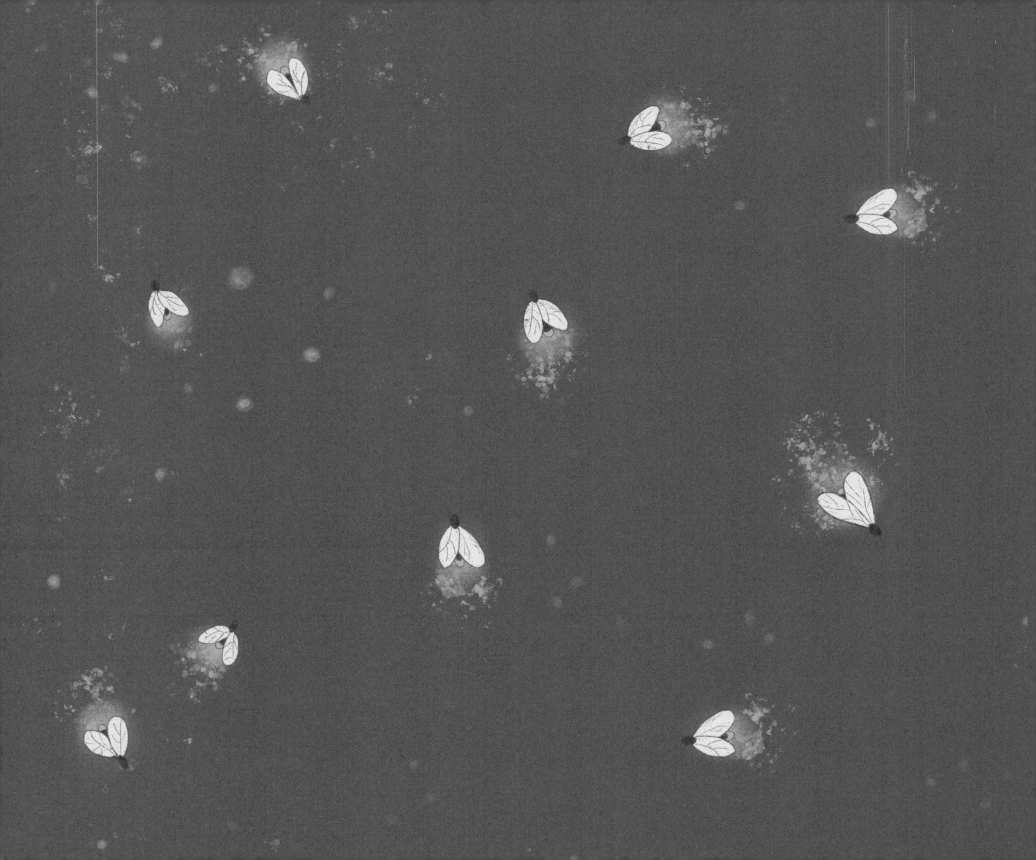

For Christian
—KM

For Tinka Plese, who showed me
the magic of sloths
—VT

Sounds True
Boulder, CO 80306

Text © 2020 Kate Messner
Illustrations © 2020 Valentina Toro

Published 2020

Book & cover design by Ranée Kahler
Cover illustration by Valentina Toro

Printed in South Korea

Library of Congress Control Number: 2020942636

10 9 8 7 6 5 4 3 2 1

SLOTH WASN'T SLEEPY

KATE MESSNER

Illustrated by
VALENTINA TORO

sounds true
BOULDER, COLORADO

One night at bedtime, Sloth wasn't sleepy.
In fact, she was the opposite of sleepy—
worked up and worried and wide awake.

"Close your eyes and rest," her mama said.

But when Sloth closed her eyes, her mind swirled with worries. Slithering snakes and sharp-taloned eagles and jaguars that prowl at night.

Sloth opened her eyes. She was wider awake than ever.

"Let's not sleep quite yet," her mother said. "We'll listen to the trees instead."

Sloth cuddled into her mama and listened.

Shush-rush, went the trees in the wind.
Shush-rush. Shush-rush.

"Can you feel the wind in your fur?"

Sloth grew still and felt for the wind.

Shush-rush. Shush-rush. It whispered
and ruffled her fur.

"Sometimes," Mama said, "I like to pretend I'm a tree. Drinking up breath from my roots to my crown, from my toes to the top of my head. Would you like to try that, too?"

Sloth nodded. But she didn't feel like a tree.

"Close your eyes," Mama said. "Now breathe in and count to four . . . and then breathe out for just as long."

Sloth closed her eyes. She counted a long, slow breath.

Whishhh... two ... three

our

two... three... four

WhOOShhh

In. All the way to the tip top of her head.
And out. All the way way down to her toes.

It made her feel quiet. She did it again.

whishhh... Two... Thre

Whoshhh

Shush-rush . . . Shush-rush . . . went the trees.

"Are you tired now?"
Mama asked.

"A little," said Sloth. "But what if I worry when I try to fall asleep?"

"Ah . . ." Mama said. "I forgot about the worries. We will have to let them go."

Sloth didn't know how to do that. But Mama said, "Close your eyes again. Imagine one of your worries."

Sloth imagined a fierce, growling
jaguar. It was terrifying. She opened
her eyes.

"Now lay that worry gently on a leaf and set it free. Let it go, way above the clouds until you can't even see it anymore."

"So long, Jaguar," Sloth whispered.

"Do you have other worries?"
Mama asked.

Sloth did. One by one, she
shrunk them down . . . and
set them free.

"So long, sharp-taloned eagle . . ."

"So long, slithering snake . . ."

When the last worry had disappeared,
Sloth took the slowest, deepest breath
of all. She filled herself up from the tips
of her toes to the very top of her head.

Whishhh

wo... three... Four...

whooshhh... Two... three... Four...

And then slowly
let it go.

She felt the cool, smooth bark of the Cecropia tree under her paws.

Whishhhh . . . two . . . three . . . four . . .
Whoooshh . . . two . . . three . . . four . . .

She felt the warm breeze in her fur.

Whishhhh . . . two . . . three . . . four . . .
Whooshhh . . . two . . . three . . .

Shush – Rush...

Shush – Rush...

Shush-rush . . . Shush-rush . . .
went the trees.

"Good night, Sloth,"
Mama whispered.

Sloth didn't answer.
She was fast asleep.

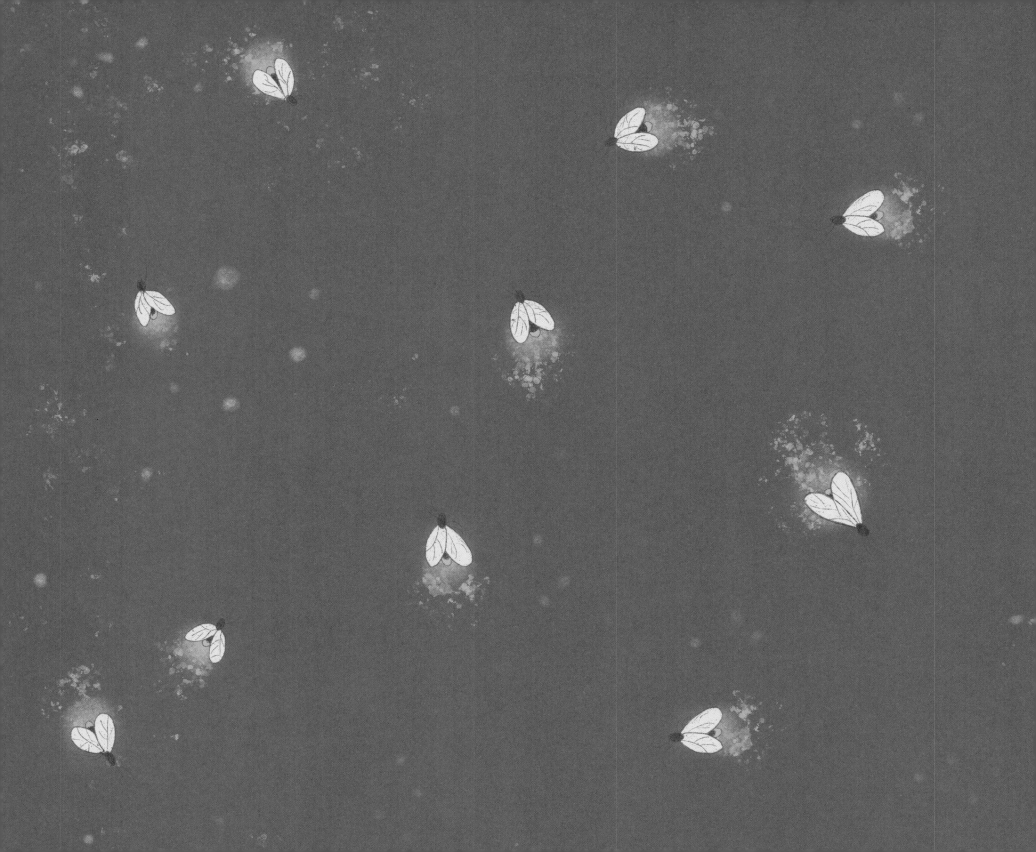

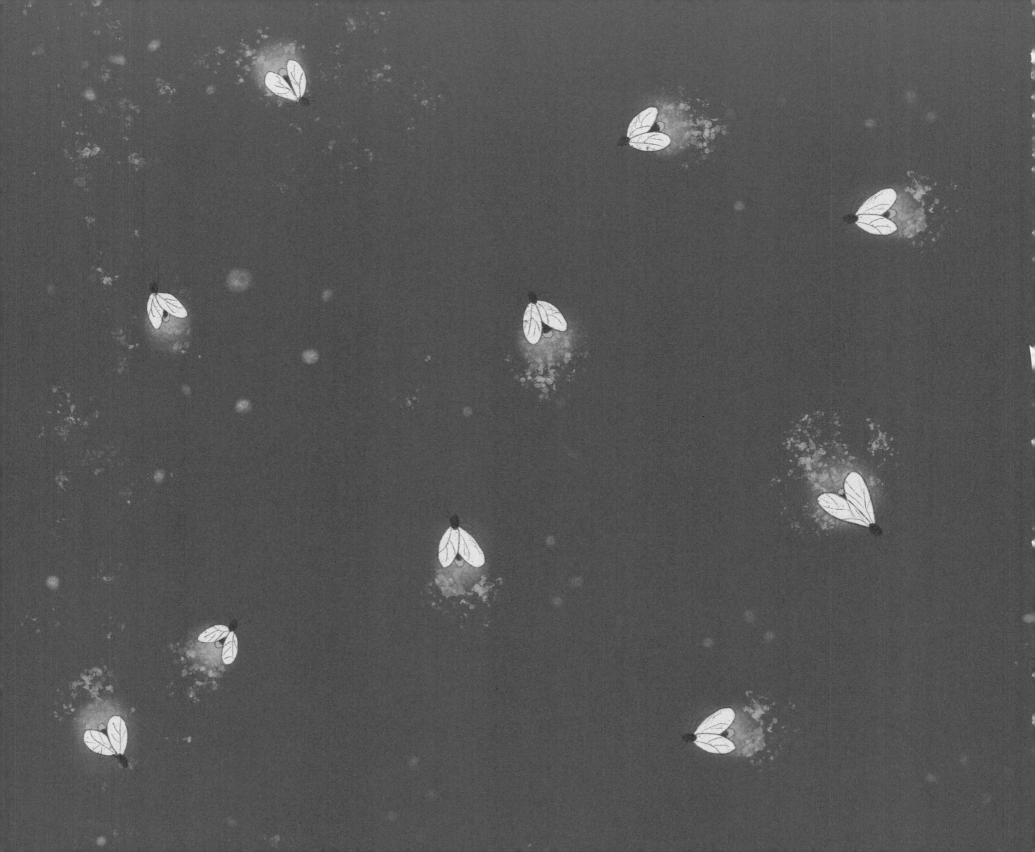